F

D0248138

08. N

02

3

26

1

Dad's New Clothes

First published in 2009
by Wayland

This paperback edition published in 2010 by Wayland

Text copyright © Louise John
Illustration copyright © Miriam Latimer

Wayland
338 Euston Road
London NW1 3BH

Wayland Australia
Level 17/207 Kent Street
Sydney, NSW 2000

Series Editor: Louise John
Cover design: Paul Cherrill
Design: D.R.ink
Consultant: Shirley Bickler

A CIP catalogue record for this book is available from the British Library.

ISBN 9780750259385 (hbk)
ISBN 9780750259422 (pbk)

Printed in China

Wayland is a division of Hachette Children's Books,
an Hachette UK Company

www.hachette.co.uk

Dad's New Clothes

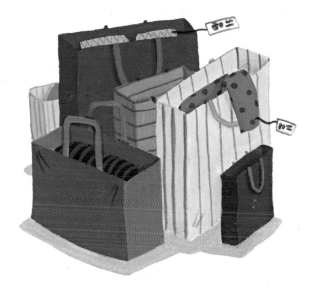

Written by Louise John
Illustrated by Miriam Latimer

WAYLAND

"New clothes for Dad,"
said Mum. "Come on!"

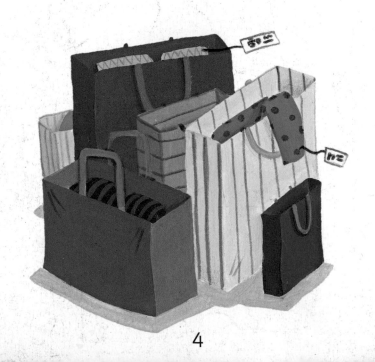

"I don't like shopping,"
said Dad.

"I like the red trousers,"
said Poppy.

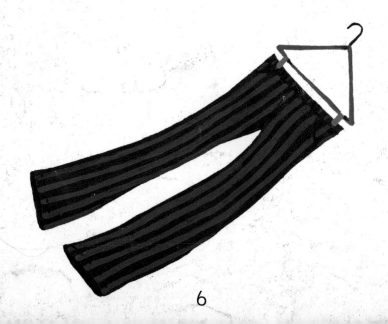

"I don't like shopping," said Dad, "and I don't like the red trousers!"

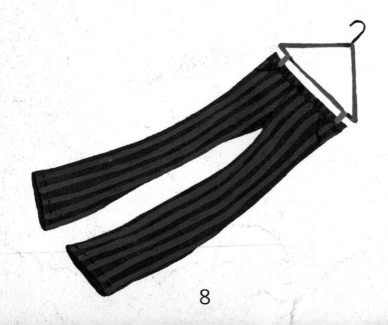

"Come and see the
socks," said Mum.
"I like the blue socks."

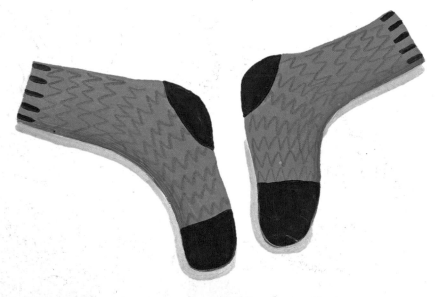

"I don't like shopping," said Dad, "and I don't like the blue socks!"

"Come and see the slippers," said Poppy. "I like the green slippers."

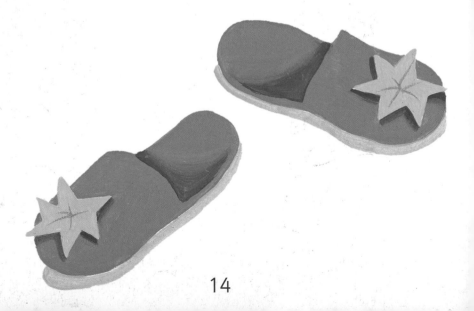

15

"No!" said Dad. "I don't like the green slippers."

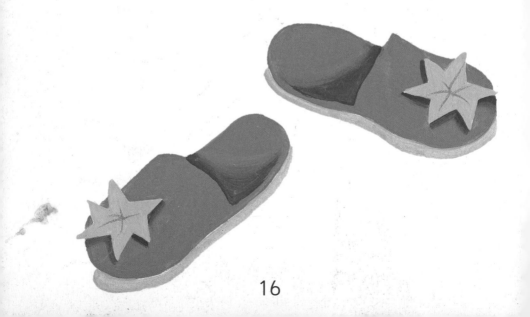

"Dad!" said Poppy.
"Come and see
the football."

19

"I don't like shopping," said Dad, "but I like the football!"

"Come ON!" said Mum.

Guiding a First Read
Dad's New Clothes

It is important to talk through the book with the child before they read it alone. This prepares them for the way the story unfolds, and allows them to enjoy the pictures as you both talk naturally, using the language they will later encounter when reading. Read them the brief overview, and then follow the suggestions below:

The high frequency words in this title are:

and	come	**Dad**	for	**I**		like
Mum	on	the	said	see		

1. Talking through the book
Mum and Poppy tried to help Dad find new clothes, but Dad kept saying, "I don't like shopping."

Let's read the title together: Dad's New Clothes.
Now let's look at the pictures. Turn to page 4.
"New clothes for Dad." said Mum. "Come on!"
Dad didn't look happy, did he?
What do you think might be saying on page 6?
Look at the picture. Poppy liked the red trousers.
Turn to page 8. Did Dad like them?

Continue through the book, guiding the discussion to fit the text, as the child looks at the illustrations.

On page 18, Poppy found something that Dad liked.
Now let's turn to the last page to see how Mum felt.

2. A first reading of the book

Ask the child to read the book independently and point carefully underneath each word (tracking), while thinking about the story.

Work with the child, prompting them. Praise their careful tracking, attempts to correct themselves and their knowledge of letters, sounds and punctuation, for example:

> **I like the way you sounded out r-e-d. Are the trousers red?**
> **Can you read that again to make Dad sound cross?**
> **You said 'shoes'. Good try. They look like shoes and the word starts with 's'. Would 'slippers' fit? Say it slowly and check the word.**

3. Follow-up activities

- Select two high frequency words, and ask the child or group to find them throughout the book. Discuss the shape of the letters and the letter sounds.

- To memorise the words, ask the child to write them in the air, then write them repeatedly on a whiteboard or on paper, leaving a space between each attempt.

4. Encourage

- Reading the book again — with expression.

- Drawing a picture based on the story.

- Writing one or two sentences using the practised words.

23

START READING is a series of highly enjoyable books for beginner readers. **The books have been carefully graded to match the Book Bands widely used in schools.** This enables readers to be sure they choose books that match their own reading ability.

Look out for the Band colour on the book in our Start Reading logo.

The Bands are:

Pink Band 1

Red Band 2

Yellow Band 3

Blue Band 4

Green Band 5

Orange Band 6

Turquoise Band 7

Purple Band 8

Gold Band 9

START READING books can be read independently or shared with an adult. They promote the enjoyment of reading through satisfying stories supported by fun illustrations.

Louise John is really the editor of Start Reading, but wanted to see how she liked writing books, too. It was quite tricky, but she found that eating lots of chocolate biscuits made her think better! She tries out her ideas on her daughter, Amelia, who tells her if they are any good or not!

Miriam Latimer enjoys illustrating and writing stories for children. She carries her sketchbook and pens with her everywhere she goes, which make her handbag very heavy. She likes to sketch people in cafés and train stations but, if they notice, she pretends to be drawing something else!